To.

June 2024

When Fur and Feather Get Together

David Margrave

Illustrated By Kim Wyly

Clovercroft Publishing

To my children,
Meredith and Andrew,
and to the child that lives in
each of our hearts.

I sat with my dad
on the top of a hill,

where the grass was tall
and the air was still.

And we talked
about animals from
fur to feather,

and what they're called when they get together.

For each animal group
he told me its name;

to my surprise they
were never the same.

What do you call
Some fish in a pool?

When lions get together
they call it a pride;

I think I'd be looking for somewhere to hide.

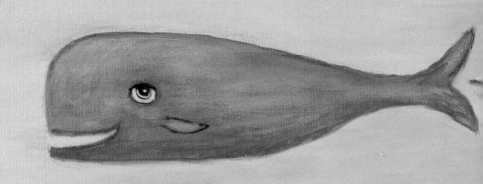

A cluster of whales
is called a pod;

So big, but so gentle,
these creatures of God.

When rhinos hang out,
it's quite a bash;

So when they get together, you call it a crash.

Hissing and honking, as they wiggle and waggle;

a gathering of geese is
called a gaggle.

Like curly white clouds
that went for a walk;

a group of sheep
is called a flock.

So worldly and wise
but still content;

an assembly of owls
is a parliament.

They're so hard to find cause
they keep you guessing;

So when you
See unicorns,
you call it a
blessing.

I leaned on my dad so warm and snug, and then climbed in his lap and gave him a hug.

I said, "Of all the groups we could be, my favorite one is our family."

David R. Margrave - Author

David Margrave grew up in Texas reading, writing stories and poems and doodling in his sketchbook. He went on to Stanford University and University of Texas Law School, and has spent his career working at a major law firm and as part of the management team of a biotech company working to develop innovative cancer treatments. Memories of reading picture books to his own two children inspired the book you are reading now.

Kim Wyly - Illustrator

Kim Wyly is a Dallas-based professional artist represented by the Elliott Yeary Gallery in Aspen. She grew up in South Texas and is bilingual. Her love of nature and her summers in Colorado inspire her paintings of abstracts and whimsical animals.

kimwyly.com

www.whenfurandfeathergettogether.com